THE POP WONDERLAND SERIES

Thumbelina

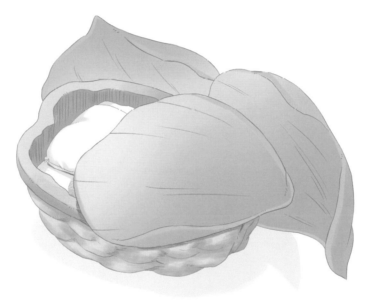

By Hans Christian Andersen

Illustrated by POP

Adapted by Michiyo Hayano

English translation by Camellia Nieh

Dark Horse Books®
Milwaukie

Once upon a time, long, long ago, a woman went to a witch to seek her help.

"If only I had a sweet little child of my own!" she said.

The witch gave the woman a magic seed.

The woman planted it, and before long, up came a little green stem with a red and yellow flower bud.

"Why, it's beautiful!" the woman marveled. She gave the little flower bud a kiss.

Immediately, the bud popped open. And lo and behold, inside the flower sat a tiny little girl!

The little girl was only as big as the woman's thumb, so the woman named her Thumbelina.

During the day, Thumbelina liked to ride around in a flower-petal boat, singing sweetly. Oh, what a beautiful voice she had!

At night, she slept in a walnut-shell bed beneath a blanket of rose petals.

One night, while Thumbelina was sleeping, a toad hopped through the window and into the room.

"Well, well! What a lovely little girl! She'll make a nice bride for my son!" the toad said. Then she snatched Thumbelina away, walnut-shell bed and all!

The next morning, when Thumbelina awoke, she was astonished to find herself on a large lily pad in the middle of a pond! There was water on all sides, and no way to get back to shore. Poor little Thumbelina began to cry.

Just then, the toad arrived with her son. "I've brought you your husband!" she told Thumbelina. "You'll live together in the mud house at the bottom of the pond!"

The toad croaked and hopped back into the pond, taking Thumbelina's walnut bed with her.

Thumbelina didn't like the idea of living in the mud under the pond. She began to cry harder than ever.

Beneath the water, the fish watched the little girl cry. "Poor little thing! Let's help her escape!" they decided.

The fish nibbled through the stem of the lily pad.

The lily pad began to drift away down the creek, and Thumbelina went with it.

That was when a friendly butterfly happened to pass. Thumbelina tied the butterfly to the lily pad with a ribbon. With the butterfly's help, the lily pad whooshed through the water.

A large beetle caught sight of Thumbelina as she traveled down the creek. "What a pretty child!" the beetle thought. He swooped down and whisked her away to show her off to his friends.

But the beetle's friends only laughed. "What a strange-looking creature! She doesn't look anything like us!"

The disappointed beetle left Thumbelina on top of a daisy and flew off.

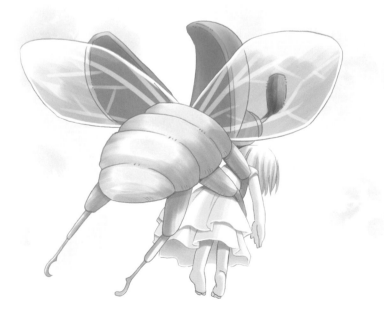

Now Thumbelina was all alone in the big forest. The little birds sang songs to cheer her up.

Thumbelina made herself a leaf hammock under a large leaf roof that kept out the rain.

She collected nectar from the flowers to eat and drank the morning dew from a leaf.

Summer passed by, and then autumn.

The trees and flowers withered and the little birds flew away. Fallen leaves crackled in the wind. Winter had come.

By now, Thumbelina's clothes were nothing but tatters, and the chilly wind blew right through them.

She wandered through the frozen forest until she came to a wheat field. In the middle of the field, she came upon a little house.

Thumbelina knocked on the door, and a field mouse answered. "Could you please give me something to eat?" Thumbelina asked.

"Oh, you poor little thing!" the field mouse exclaimed. "Come inside where it's warm!"

From then on, Thumbelina lived with the kindly field mouse.

A mole lived next door to the field mouse's house.

When he met Thumbelina, he fell in love with her immediately and asked her to marry him.

The field mouse thought it was a good idea. "Mr. Mole is rich!" she told Thumbelina. "You'll have a good life if you marry him."

But the mole didn't like sunlight or pretty flowers, and Thumbelina didn't love him back.

There was a tunnel between the field mouse's house and the mole's house.

One day, Thumbelina came across a fallen swallow in the tunnel.

"Why, you poor thing!" Thumbelina exclaimed. "You're one of the birds who sang to me so sweetly in the summer!"

Thumbelina stroked the swallow's feathers, remembering the warm summer sun and the forest filled with green.

Then she covered the bird with a fallen leaf and brought him water to drink in a flower petal. Little by little, the swallow began to recover.

"Thank you," he said. "I think I'll be able to fly again, thanks to you."

The swallow had been flying off to a warmer country with his friends when he'd hurt his wing and had been unable to continue his journey.

Finally, the warm glow of spring came again. By now, the swallow was all better.

"Will you come away with me to a warmer place?" the swallow asked.

"I'm afraid I can't," Thumbelina told him. She knew the old field mouse would be sad if she left.

"Then I'll have to go alone. Goodbye!" the swallow called.

Thumbelina watched for a long time as the swallow flew away.

N ow, we've got to prepare for your wedding!" the field mouse
chuckled happily.

The mole came to visit often. He was very pleased about the
wedding, too.

But Thumbelina wasn't the slightest bit happy.

She sighed, remembering the bright sunlight and gentle breezes
of the world above.

F inally, the day of the wedding arrived. Thumbelina was filled with sadness. When she married the mole, she would never again see the sunlight or flowers.

"Goodbye, sun!" Thumbelina said, hugging a red flower that grew up out of the earth. "Goodbye, everyone!"

Just then, Thumbelina heard the sound of chirping overhead.

It was her friend the swallow! Once again, he invited her to join him on his journey.

This time, Thumbelina decided to go.

The swallow flew off with Thumbelina on his back. Together, they soared over forests and villages.

Finally, the swallow came to rest next to a blue pond. All around, there were beautiful flowers in every color of the rainbow.

The swallow set Thumbelina down on a flower with petals as white as snow.

Thumbelina was astonished to discover another tiny person sitting in the middle of the flower.

He was the Prince of the Flowers, and he had shimmering wings and a crown of gold.

"Won't you marry me and become Queen of the Flowers?" the Prince asked Thumbelina.

That was how Thumbelina came to marry the Prince of the Flowers.

(When the swallow heard, he was a little bit sad, because he had loved Thumbelina as well.)

Thumbelina was given a pair of white wings, and she and the Prince flew from flower to flower.

And they lived happily ever after, in a land filled with sunlight and flowers.

Look for these other POP WONDERLAND books from Dark Horse Books:

Little Red Riding Hood (Fall 2009)

Alice's Adventures in Wonderland (Spring 2010)

Cinderella (Summer 2010)

PUBLISHER: Mike Richardson EDITOR: Robert Simpson ASSISTANT EDITOR: Rachel Edidin DESIGNER: Heidi Whitcomb

POP WONDERLAND: Thumbelina
Illustration copyright © POP 2007 • Text copyright © Michiyo Hayano 2007 • Planned and designed by MASTERPIECE, Inc. • All rights reserved.
Original Japanese edition published by POPLAR Publishing Co., Ltd., Tokyo • English translation rights directly arranged with POPLAR Publishing Co., Ltd.

Cover painting by POP • English translation by Camellia Nieh
Special thanks to Janna Morishima, Michael Gombos, and Annie Gullion.

Published by Dark Horse Books, a division of Dark Horse Comics, Inc. • 10956 SE Main Street, Milwaukie OR 97222
darkhorse.com

First Dark Horse Books Edition: June 2009 • ISBN 978-1-59582-268-0 • Printed in China

1 3 5 7 9 10 8 6 4 2

Publisher MIKE RICHARDSON • Executive Vice President NEIL HANKERSON • Chief Financial Officer TOM WEDDLE • Vice President Of Publishing RANDY STRADLEY • Vice President Of Business Development MICHAEL MARTENS • Vice President Of Marketing, Sales, And Licensing ANITA NELSON • Vice President Of Product Development DAVID SCROGGY • Vice President Of Information Technology DALE LAFOUNTAIN Director Of Purchasing DARLENE VOGEL • General Counsel KEN LIZZI • Editorial Director DAVEY ESTRADA • Senior Managing Editor SCOTT ALLIE • Senior Books Editor, Dark Horse Books CHRIS WARNER Senior Books Editor, M Press/Dh Press ROBERT SIMPSON • Executive Editor DIANA SCHUTZ • Director Of Design And Production CARY GRAZZINI • Art Director LIA RIBACCHI • Director Of Scheduling CARA NIECE